W9-BPK-458

Curious George®
Tadpole Trouble

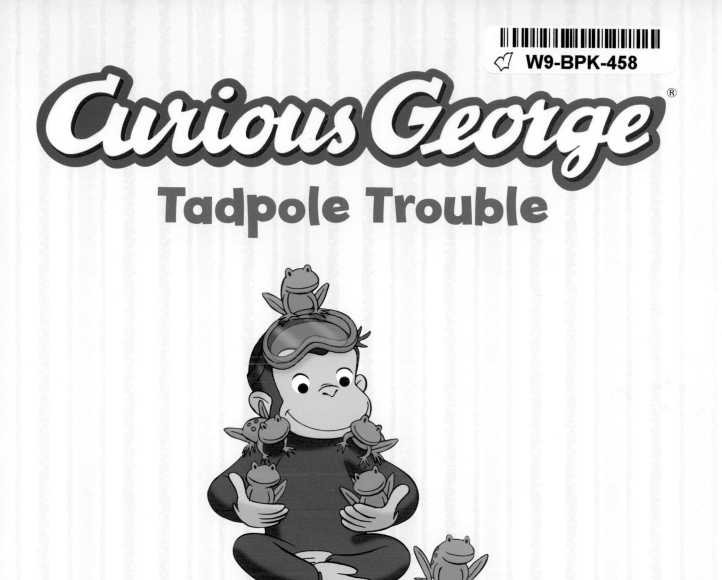

Adaptation by Mark London Williams
Based on the TV series teleplay written by Bruce Akiyama

Houghton Mifflin Company, Boston

Copyright © 2007 Universal Studios. Curious George and related characters, created by Margret and H. A. Rey, are copyrighted and trademarked by Houghton Mifflin Company and used under license. CURIOUS GEORGE television series licensed by Universal Studios Licensing LLLP. All rights reserved.

The PBS KIDS logo is a registered trademark of PBS and is used with permission.

For information about permission to reproduce selections from this book, write to Permissions, Houghton Mifflin Company, 215 Park Avenue South, New York, New York 10003.

Library of Congress Cataloging-in-Publication Data
Williams, Mark London.
Curious George, tadpole trouble / adaptation by Mark London Williams ; based on the teleplay written by Bruce Akiyama.
p. cm.
ISBN-13: 978-0-618-77712-9 (pbk. : alk. paper)
ISBN-10: 0-618-77712-1 (pbk. : alk. paper)
I. Akiyama, Bruce. II. Curious George (Television program) III. Title. IV. Title: Tadpole trouble.
PZ7.W66697Cur 2007
[E]—dc22
2006036469

Design by Joyce White

www.houghtonmifflinbooks.com

Printed in Singapore
TWP 10 9 8 7 6 5 4 3 2

George was exploring a lake with his friend Bill. George was a good
explorer, and always very curious.

He was especially curious about tadpoles.

Bill told George he could be in charge of the tadpoles they found.

George took tadpole-watching very seriously. He watched them swim in their glass bowl. He fed them boiled lettuce.

He took them for a swim in the lake. At the time it seemed like good exercise for tadpoles.

When the tadpoles did not come back, George started to worry. What would Bill say? He had to find them.

George spent hours at the lake. He found turtles, and water beetles, and minnows. But no tadpoles.

Every time George would visit the lake he would look for the tadpoles. Several weeks went by.

Finally he found something that looked like a tadpole — but it had legs, and almost no tail. George let it go.

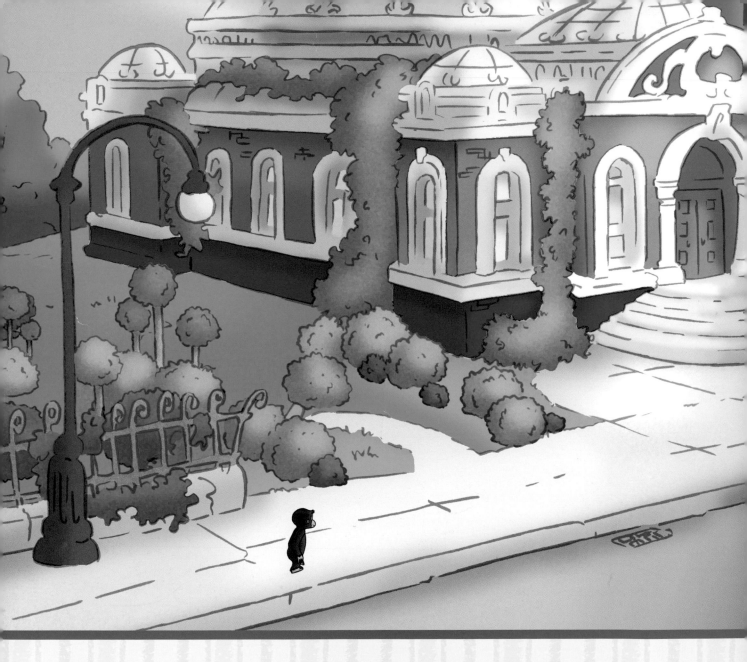

A few weeks after that, George took a walk in the city to think about his tadpole problem. He was going back to the lake soon. Bill would be very disappointed if George had lost the tadpoles.

George walked so long, he found himself in front of the museum. He saw a
butterfly that reminded him of being at the lake. He followed it.

The butterfly flew into the museum and George kept following, past all kinds of exhibits.

There was a special display about creatures that live around lakes. George knew about many of them, like turtles, minnows, lizards . . . and tadpoles!

The picture of the baby tadpole reminded him of his own tadpoles. Next to it was one of the funny creatures George had seen in the lake. It had legs and a smaller tail.

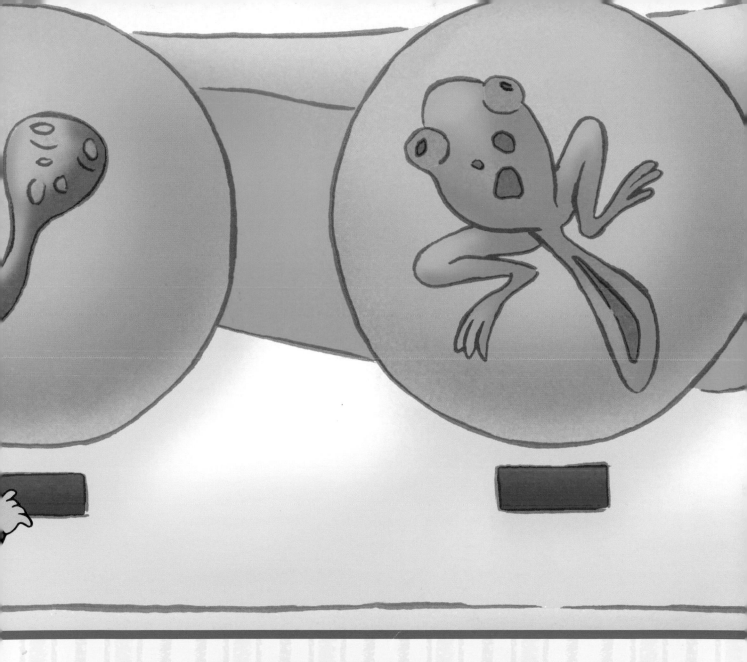

Now he understood! The creatures with legs were tadpoles, too! His friends had not vanished. They were just changing and growing up. George was so excited, he left the museum without finishing the exhibit tour.

As soon as George got back to the lake, he looked for his missing friends. Especially the ones with little legs and almost no tails.

But they were not there, either. This time George could find only . . . frogs! Lots and lots of frogs!

"What a good idea, George," Bill said, seeing the empty jar.

"You decided to release the tadpoles into their natural habitat so we could watch them grow into frogs. You're not only curious—you're smart, too!"

"Let's take a picture of you and the frogs together, George. Smile!"

A FROG'S LIFE

Many animals change body shapes over the course of their life cycles.
Frogs are one kind. Can you think of any others?★

Here are the main stages of a frog's life, out of order.
Number them one to four in the proper order.

4

**FROG
(12-16 WEEKS)**

1

**EGGS
(BEFORE HATCHING)**

3

**TADPOLE WITH LEGS
(6-9 WEEKS)**

2

**TADPOLE
(BIRTH-4 WEEKS)**

★ Here are some: mosquitoes, butterflies, ladybugs, silkworms, mealworms, ants, cicadas